Mermaid KINGDOM

Mermaid Kingdom is published by Stone Arch Books
A Capstone Imprint
1710 Roe Crest Drive
North Mankato, Minnesota 56003
www.mycapstone.com

Library of Congress Cataloging-in-Publication Data
Gurtler, Janet, author.
Rachel's worry / by Janet Gurtler ; illustrated by Katie Wood.
pages cm. -- (Mermaid kingdom)

Summary: Rachel is worried that she has done something to upset her human friend, Owen, because lately he has not come to visit her in Neptunia — but it turns out that the truth could put an end to their friendship completely.

ISBN 978-1-4965-2607-6 (hardcover) -- ISBN 978-1-4965-2609-0 (pbk.) -- ISBN 978-1-4965-2611-3 (ebook pdf)

1. Mermaids--Juvenile fiction. 2. Moving, Household--Juvenile fiction. 3. Dating (Social customs)--Juvenile fiction. 4. Friendship--Juvenile fiction. [1. Mermaids--Fiction. 2. Moving, Household--Fiction. 3. Dating (Social customs)--Fiction. 4. Friendship--Fiction.] I. Wood, Katie, 1981- illustrator. II. Title. III. Series: Gurtler, Janet. Mermaid kingdom.
PZ7.G9818Rb 2016
813.6--dc23
[Fic]

2015021994

Designer: Alison Thiele

Artistic Elements: Shutterstock

Printed in the United States of America in
North Mankato, Minnesota.
092015 009221CGS16

Rachel's Worry

by Janet Gurtler

illustrated by Katie Wood

STONE ARCH BOOKS

a capstone imprint

Mermaid Life

Mermaid Kingdom refers to all the kingdoms in the sea, including Neptunia, Caspian, Hercules, Titania, and Nessland. Each kingdom has a king and queen who live in a castle. Merpeople live in caves.

Mermaids get their legs on their thirteenth birthdays at the stroke of midnight. It's a celebration when the mermaid makes her first voyage onto land. After their thirteenth birthdays, mermaids can go on land for short periods of time but must be very careful.

If a mermaid goes on land before her thirteenth birthday, she will get her legs early and never get her tail back. She will lose all memories of being a mermaid and will be human forever.

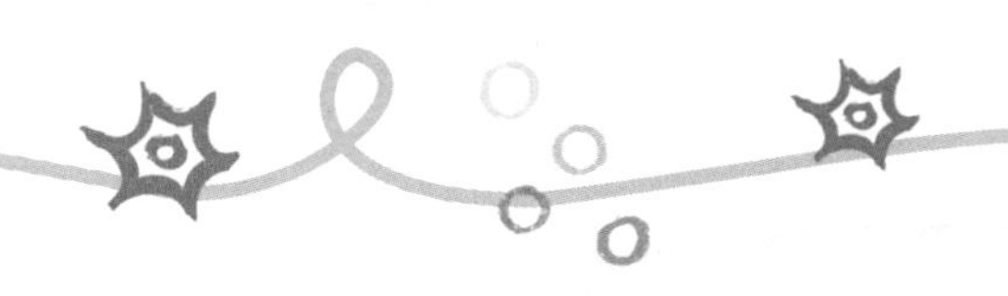

Mermaids are able to stay on land with legs for no more than forty-eight hours. Any longer and they will not be able to get their tails back and will be human forever. They will lose all memories of being a mermaid.

If they fall in love, merpeople and humans can marry and have babies (with special permission from the king and queen of their kingdom). Their babies are half-human and half-merperson. However, this love must be the strongest love possible in order for it to be approved by the king and queen.

Half-human mermaids are able to go on land indefinitely and can change back to a mermaid anytime. However, they are not allowed to tell other humans about the mermaid world unless they have special permission from the king and queen.

Chapter One

My stomach hurt from worrying about my best friend, Owen, a human I'd met onshore when I lived at Caspian Castle. I could tell something was wrong with him, and I needed to find out what so I could try to help him feel better.

I chomped on my lip like it was a salty seaweed snack as my friend Shyanna and I swam out of Walrus Waterpark. Cora, our other friend, had left a few minutes earlier, swimming off in the opposite direction.

Shyanna giggled as we swam past a bloom of jellyfish. Her beautiful tail sparkled and reflected off their translucent skin. She waved at them and then turned back to me. When she saw my face, her expression softened. "What's wrong, Rachel?" Shyanna asked.

"To tell the truth, I'm worried about Owen," I told her.

Shyanna stopped swimming. "What's wrong with Owen? Is he sick? Does he have one of those human diseases like chicken pox? Wait. Has he been around chickens? Have you ever seen real live chickens? They're as cute as sea cucumbers."

I was too troubled to even smile at Shyanna's excitement. "He's not sick, but Owen hasn't come to visit Neptunia in a long time, even though he can, thanks to the special merman powers the King and Queen granted him. And when I go to shore to visit, he doesn't seem happy to see me," I told her.

"Did you ask him what's wrong?" Shy asked.

My cheeks heated up. I hadn't. I'd been trying to think if I'd done something wrong, something to make him mad. I sighed. "I'm kind of afraid to."

Shyanna swam close and hugged me. "You need to ask, Rachel," she said. "Talk to him. And it's Friday so you're going to see him today, right?"

"Yeah," I said with a nod. Every Friday I swam to shore and visited Owen. Since I was half-human, I could go on land whenever I wanted and change back to a mermaid anytime.

"So ask!" she said.

As if sensing my gloomy mood, a clown fish started flipping around in front of me, trying to make me laugh. I smiled but glanced toward the exit of our castle. "I'm heading to Platypus Island now," I said.

"Alone?" Shyanna asked. "I wish I could come, but I'm meeting my mom at the Fish Factory, and then we're going to visit Pearl Sparkles."

I nodded. "It's okay. I have a route worked out. It's fast and safe, and I've never run into trouble."

Shyanna frowned for a moment. "Okay, but be careful," she warned me. Then she grinned her warm, friendly smile and patted my shoulder. "And try not to be nervous. If you ask Owen, I'm sure he'll tell you what's wrong."

I nodded. Swimming to shore alone didn't worry me. I'd done it enough times by now. It was Owen who worried me. I hoped Shyanna was right and once I talked to him, everything would go back to normal.

I waved goodbye to Shyanna and swam out the gates of Neptunia. Before I knew it, I'd reached the Octopi guards outside Platypus Island. They nodded as I passed. They were used to seeing me heading to shore to visit.

My stomach fluttered with nerves as I neared the shoreline. My head poked through the top of the water, and my lungs switched to breathing in oxygen from air rather than the water. As I reached shallow water, I felt pebbles on my tail. It began to tingle and transform, and in moments, human legs took its place. I now wore shorts the same color as my fin, and I stood up and ran to grab the shoes I'd stored behind a bush close to the beach.

Excitement mixing with worry gave me a burst of energy, and I ran faster than usual toward my meeting spot with Owen. A smile tugged up my lips up as I ducked around branches, climbing over rocks and sticks. The scent of the trees and grass, so different from the ocean, filled my nose.

Finally I reached the spot where Owen met me on Fridays. I crossed my fingers, hoping he'd be back to his happy self — or at least trust me enough to tell me what was bothering him.

I parted the branches and stepped through. Our meeting place was empty.

Nothing. No sign of Owen.

I walked farther out in the field, wondering if he was running late. But Owen was never late. Never. I glanced around again, but he was nowhere to be seen.

My mouth began to quiver. Owen wasn't showing up. He didn't want to talk to me. I swallowed and thought about going out after him. But he hadn't shown up. I couldn't chase after him. If he'd wanted to talk to me, he'd have come to meet me.

The minutes ticked by slowly, and my body felt heavier with every passing second. I sat on a big rock, waiting, but Owen never came.

Chapter Two

A shark held Owen between his teeth. I held his leg, pulling as hard as I could, but I couldn't manage to free him.

"OWEN!" I yelled.

Suddenly there was a huge thump, followed by pain in my tail. My eyes flew open. I'd flipped myself right off my bed and landed on the floor. I'd been asleep; it was just a nightmare.

I sighed as reality roared into my sleepy head. Owen had stood me up! He didn't like me anymore.

I swallowed and swam up from the floor, trying to think happy mermaid thoughts, but it was no use. I was as blue as a hundred-foot whale.

"Rachel!" Dad called from outside my bedroom. "The mergirls are here. Are you awake? Can I send them up?"

I rubbed the sleep out of my eyes. "Sure!" I replied. Almost as soon as the word was out of my mouth, Shyanna and Cora raced into my room.

"Hey, sleepyhead," Shyanna said, laughing. "How come you're still in bed?"

"I slept in," I said. "I couldn't get to sleep last night." I swam toward my door to avoid giving more detail. "Come on, I'm starving. Let's go to the kitchen and get some food. I'm sure my dad made extra breakfast."

Shyanna sped up beside me and bumped my fin with hers. "So?" she said pointedly. "How did it go with Owen? Is everything okay between you guys now?"

My lip trembled. I swallowed, but it felt like a piece of coral was stuck in my throat. Ignoring Shyanna's question, I hurried to the kitchen where, as expected, Dad was frying up breakfast. Shrimp fries. Enough for all of us.

Dad lifted his spatula in a wave when we entered. "Hey, mergirls, I hope you're hungry," he said.

"Always!" Shyanna said.

Cora swam close to me and tapped me on my shoulder. "What's wrong, Rachel?"

My lips wobbled and tears threatened to spill out. I waved my hands in front of my face, trying to smile even though I wanted to cry. Dad watched me, looking worried.

"What happened?" Shy asked. "Did something happen during your trip to shore yesterday?"

"Is something wrong with Owen?" Cora asked.

"What's wrong with my favorite daughter?" Dad asked at the same time.

Cora and Shyanna each reached for one of my hands and squeezed it. Dad watched, flipping over the shrimp. I couldn't even enjoy the delicious smell of the special breakfast. Sadness made my tail droop.

"Owen didn't show up," I said, and a tear slipped out. Shyanna quickly reached for it and held it in her hand, then grabbed a container to slip my tear inside. Mermaid tears are full of mermaid magic, so it was important not to waste a single one.

Cora, Shyanna, and my dad all started firing off questions at once:

"Did you go to his house?"

"Did you look for him?"

"Why didn't you tell me?"

I shook my head and refused to look at any of them. "He obviously didn't want to see me, so I wasn't going to make it worse by chasing all over after him." My chin dropped to my chest as I finally faced the truth I'd been trying to avoid. "He doesn't like me anymore, and he clearly doesn't want to be my friend."

My dad scoffed at that. "What's not to like?" He swam over to the cupboard and grabbed some shell plates. Then he swam quickly back to the stove to start dishing out breakfast.

"Exactly," Shyanna said, swimming over to help my dad set out some Plant Life veggies on the plates. "He's your best friend, Rachel. You've known him longer than you've known us, and we love you more with every passing day!"

Cora swam over to help my dad too. "Owen loves when you visit him onshore. Especially on Friday. He told Justin that."

I glanced over and saw her cheeks turn a little pink. Justin was one of Owen's human friends. We'd met him when we'd visited Owen on land, and it seemed like Cora had developed a bit of a crush on him. She turned quickly away and grabbed a jug of clam juice.

"And Owen loves visiting the ocean too," Cora continued. "You're his best friend, and he's yours. Well, along with me and Shy." She smiled as she put out shell cups for the clam juice.

Dad clapped his hands together. "All right! Let's eat." He pointed at the feast on the table. "Rachel, you're too hard on yourself. Owen's a special human and getting to use a mertail is really important to him — as are you. It has to be something else. Did you two have a fight?"

I shook my head. "No. That's the thing. I can't pinpoint anything. I've gone over it and over it, but he's been acting funny for a few weeks. Maybe he doesn't like the fact that I'm a mermaid anymore. Maybe he doesn't want friends like me. I'm so different from all his other human friends."

"Nonsense," Shyanna, Cora, and my dad all said at the same time. If I weren't so worried, I'd have thought it was kind of funny the way they kept talking in sync.

"Listen, Rachel, I know you're sensitive, but Owen thinks you're the catfish's meow," Cora added.

"Not anymore," I muttered, hanging my head again.

"Maybe he was in an accident," Shyanna suggested.

"More likely he got in trouble, and his parents wouldn't let him go out," Dad said. "Swim up to the table, mergirls, and fill up your plates."

Cora loaded her plate. "Let's all go to shore. We can ask Justin if he knows anything. Um, I mean, we can talk to his friends. We'll find out what's going on. We can make lots of guesses, but how well do we really understand human behavior?" She shoved a huge mouthful of shrimp into her mouth and giggled. "Mmm. This is delicious, Mr. Marlin."

I shoved a shrimp into my own mouth and watched Cora. I had a sneaking suspicion her desire to go back to shore had something to do with Justin.

"It is a good idea," Shyanna agreed. "Thanks for cooking for us, Mr. Marlin." She helped herself to a large helping of Plant Life with her shrimp and turned to me. "Let's go get an answer."

"But we're supposed to go play with the dolphins later," I pointed out. "And I know how much you love that."

"It's okay," Shy said. "We need to find out what's really going on with Owen. There's no way he doesn't want to be your friend anymore. That makes no sense at all."

I glanced at my dad. He nodded. "It's okay with me, but you mergirls better check with your mothers," he said to my friends. "After we finish our feast."

We all ate up, and I listened halfheartedly as my friends chatted with my dad about what Queen Kenna was up to these days. Nerves flipped around my stomach, and I could barely follow along.

After we'd cleaned up, Cora and Shyanna took out their shell phones to call their caves.

"Please, Mom," Cora begged when it was her turn. "It's really important that I go to shore to help

Rachel. I can ask Cassie to look after baby Jewel."

She listened and then hung up the shell phone and looked at me, a little panic in her eyes.

"You sure seem anxious to go to shore," my dad said with a wink.

"For Rachel, of course," Cora said. "I'm supposed to babysit because my mom is taking my other sisters to the merdoctor, and my dad is working." Cora dialed again and breathed a sigh of relief when Cassie agreed to babysit. Then she called her mom back and told her the good news.

"I don't have long," Cora said when she finally hung up for good. "I have to be back in two hours, or I'm in the trouble of my life. Like huge."

"No problem," I told her. "That gives us lots of time. I promise."

"Okay!" Shyanna said, swimming to my side and linking arms with Cora and me. "We're all set."

Dad swam with us to the front of the cave and watched us swim off. "Have fun, mergirls!" he called.

"Swim safe, and, Rachel, remember to check the time when you're on land, so you don't overstay your visit! You don't want to get Cora in trouble when she's doing you a favor by going to shore with you."

"I won't, Dad!" I called back. As a half-human, I could stay onshore as long as I wanted, while Shyanna and Cora could be on land as long as forty-eight hours before their tails grew back. But despite all that, Cora had limited time. We needed to get home in two hours. I'd promised.

"Come on," Cora said. She sped out in front of us and did a figure eight so quickly her purple tail was a blur. "Let's go find out what's wrong with Owen."

Chapter Three

We raced through the ocean, passing by other castles and occasionally seeing other merboys and mergirls we recognized. We waved but kept moving quickly so they wouldn't swim over to say hello. I didn't want to waste any of our precious time.

But suddenly I spotted a problem. Up ahead, only about one hundred feet away, there was a frenzy of short-fin mako sharks swimming in circles.

"Oh, no!" I cried, my eyes going as wide as sand dollars. "Look!"

"Come on," Shyanna said. She grabbed my hand and quickly darted behind a giant blue whale. Cora swam close behind. The whale blinked kindly, and we rubbed up against him while the sharks swam closer and closer.

I held my breath, terrified. These were the same kind of sharks that had killed my mom years ago. Ocean life was truly breathtaking, but it was also dangerous.

Once, when Shyanna had gone to shore looking for a magical cure for her sore throat, we'd swum straight into a pack of sharks. She'd had to rescue me when I froze as the sharks approached, their pointed teeth bared. Shyanna had made me sing with her, and the blend of our voices had mesmerized the sharks and saved our lives.

"I'm so glad I haven't run into them again since that last time with you," I whispered to Shyanna as our new whale friend kept us camouflaged and safe from harm.

Fortunately, this time the sharks swam off without spotting us. "This is why I worry about you when you come to shore alone," Shyanna told me.

We thanked the whale and promised to bring him some special krill the next time we came to shore, then swam off toward Platypus Island.

As soon as we got close to the beach, I spotted Owen and his friends, Justin, Mitchel, and Morgan, standing in the field just past the tree line that separated the land from the beach. The boys were kicking around a black-and-white ball on the grass. I looked at Owen's face from the distance. He wore a giant smile, which made my heart both happy and sad. He never looked like that when he looked at me these days, but at least he was happy now!

"That's a soccer ball," Cora whispered. She loved all water sports in the ocean and had made it her mission to learn about all the human ones ever since she'd gotten her legs on her thirteenth birthday and started coming to shore with me.

Shyanna, Cora, and I tried not to make any noise as our tails tingled, and we got our legs. Then we all grabbed the shoes we kept stashed onshore and started through the trees.

"Shhh," Cora whispered as she took off in the lead. She was the fastest swimmer and the fastest on land too. "Let's sneak up and surprise them." Her eyes sparkled like stars above the ocean.

We crept closer, and all at once Cora emerged from the tree line. "Boo!" she shouted.

I hung back a little, watching Owen's reaction. His eyes immediately met mine, and for a moment, he dropped his gaze. When he glanced up again, he was smiling, but the usual spark wasn't in his eyes. My stomach flopped like a flappy fish.

Cora jumped up as high as she could with gravity and legs instead of water and a tail. Shyanna jumped too, and both of them whooped out loud, caught up in the excitement of being on land with humans — cute boy ones at that.

Cora ran straight for the black-and-white ball and kicked it high in the air.

"Nice kick!" Justin shouted, taking off after the ball.

Cora giggled and blushed, proving that my hunch was right. She had a crush on him!

I smiled and watched as Morgan and Owen chased after Justin. Cora followed. With an apologetic glance at me, as if she couldn't help herself, Shyanna took off running too. Mitchel whooped and then followed behind her.

I stayed close to the tree line and quietly watched the fun. The girls tried to keep up, but the boys raced around them, passing the ball to one another using their feet.

I didn't mind that Shyanna and Cora were playing along. There was still time to talk to Owen. Besides, it didn't look like the boys were in any hurry to stop and talk. Owen glanced at me from time to time, but he didn't come over.

Finally Justin kicked the ball close to me and raced after it, his brownish-blond hair standing straight up in the wind. His nice white teeth flashed a delighted grin as he ran toward me. He looked as happy and friendly as a dancing dolphin.

I stepped out of his way and saw Owen running closer to me, closing in on Justin from behind. Cora screeched, trying to catch up. I glanced over at her, and when I looked back, Owen was standing right in front of me, panting and out of breath.

"Uh . . . I'm really sorry I couldn't make it yesterday, Rachel," Owen said. He glanced away, his eyes following the ball as Justin kicked it high in the air. "I wanted to let you know so you wouldn't come all that way for nothing, but uh . . . I had no way of reaching you."

Owen shuffled his feet a little and stared down at the grass. "Our Internet doesn't exactly work in the ocean, and I can't reach you on a shell phone." He lifted a shoulder and shrugged as if it were no big deal. As if it didn't much matter to him one way or the other.

I waited for more. For him to tell me why he couldn't make it, why he was acting so distant, why he didn't like me anymore. But Owen turned away without a second glance and took off after the ball.

I stared after him, feeling like my heart had been pierced by a fishhook.

Chapter Four

A few minutes later, Cora ran close to me. She stopped and bumped my hip with hers. "So you and Owen talked and now everything's okay?" she said. She didn't really seem to be listening for my answer. She was too busy watching Justin and the ball. She seemed to have forgotten all about her offer to talk to the other boys and help me figure out what was wrong with Owen.

I shrugged, but Cora grabbed my hand and pulled me, running so I had no choice but to follow to keep up. "Come on, this game is so much fun!" she exclaimed.

I dropped Cora's hand and came to a halt on the grass as she chased after her crush. Now I felt even worse. Cora didn't care, and Owen didn't care. What was wrong? Was it me? Was I doing something to make my friends turn away from me?

Just then, Shyanna ran to my side. "Are you okay, Rachel?" she asked. "Did you and Owen talk? Is everything okay? He told you what's wrong, right?"

I shook my head, feeling miserable. Shy and I both looked over to where Owen was running, his head thrown back with laughter.

"But he seems fine," Shyanna said. "He doesn't seem mad at you. I mean, yeah, he's obviously into the soccer game right now, but you know he loves sports. He's like Cora. He gets caught up and forgets everything else."

I nodded, wishing she were right.

"Come on!" Shyanna encouraged. "Join in the fun. Everything's okay!"

I wanted to believe her, but my heart didn't agree. "I don't know," I said cautiously, but Shyanna ignored my protests and pulled me into the game.

I halfheartedly joined in and kept an eye on Owen. He seemed to run off in the opposite direction whenever I got close enough to talk to him. Something was definitely off, and I seemed to be the only person who could see it. Or maybe I was just the only person Owen wasn't happy around.

"Let's take a break," Justin suggested after awhile. He plunked down on the grass, and everyone else followed his lead.

I moved closer to Owen and sat down next to him, but he quickly jumped up to grab the soccer ball. When he sat back down, he made sure to do it on the other side of the circle. I plucked up some grass in my hand and squished the blades between my fingers, noticing how my fingers turned green.

"Our swim team is going to the championships next weekend," Justin announced.

"Our club has a good chance to win the Castle . . . um . . . championships," Cora said. Unlike Owen, the rest of the boys had no idea we were mermaids.

"Wait a minute, I thought you girls didn't swim," Morgan said. "I've never seen any of you in the ocean. I thought you were afraid of the water."

Cora's eyes opened wide, realizing her mistake.

Luckily, Mitchel didn't seem to notice anything out of the ordinary. "You wanna race?" he asked with a smile.

Cora, Shyanna, and I exchanged nervous glances. We couldn't race the boys. In fact, as mergirls, we couldn't swim in front of humans at all. As soon as we were in water, our legs would disappear and our glorious sparkly tails would be on display. Other than Owen, who had special permission from the King and Queen of Neptunia and knew about mermaids, humans were not allowed to see our tails.

"Uh . . ." Cora said. "I can't. I . . . uh . . . I thought you meant um . . ." she appeared to be searching for the right word.

"Did you mean your track team?" Owen said quietly.

"Yeah, exactly," Cora agreed quickly, glancing down at her legs. She stretched them out in front of her and wiggled them around. "I was talking about running track. The running championships."

"Yeah?" Justin grinned his playful grin and jumped to his feet. "I'll race you."

Shyanna and I both shook our heads, but Cora's gaze was focused on Justin. She jumped up, unable to resist a challenge.

"Cora," Shyanna said warningly. We both knew Cora wasn't nearly as fast on her legs as she was with her tail. She hadn't been thirteen for very long and was still getting used to her legs.

But there was no stopping Cora. She was off and running, and Justin took off after her. They hadn't gone far when suddenly we heard a crunch, and then Cora dropped to her knees, yelling and grabbing at her leg.

"Ow!" Cora yelped as the rest of us jumped up and ran over. When Justin noticed she wasn't behind him anymore, he turned and quickly ran back to her.

Cora rubbed at her leg. "It's nothing," she said, but it was obvious from the look on her face that it hurt — a lot. She tried to stand up and walk but collapsed to the ground.

I glanced up. The sun was moving east. We'd lost some time when we'd hidden from the sharks, and we needed to start moving to get Cora home on time. If she was late, she wouldn't be coming back to the shore for a long, long time. She'd be devastated.

"Just sit and rest for a while before you try to move," Justin said.

Shyanna caught my eye. "We have to get going soon," she said, a nervous crack in her voice. "Cora has a curfew."

"We'll walk you home," the boys offered. Mitchel and Morgan each took one of Cora's arms and helped lift her to her feet.

Shyanna and I looked at each other. The boys couldn't walk us home — not to Mermaid Kingdom — and we couldn't let them see where we were going.

"No, it's okay," Shyanna said. "We'll take her." We tried to force them out of the way, but they didn't let go of Cora.

I glanced at the sun again. We really did need to get to the shore. We didn't have time to wait for Cora's foot to feel better, and we couldn't let the boys come with us to the ocean. They'd see the truth.

I glanced at Owen. "Help," I mouthed.

Owen smiled, and in that moment, he looked just like my old friend. My heart sped up. It was the first time he'd looked at me like that in weeks. Maybe things would be okay after all.

"Hey, guys," Owen said to his friends. "The girls are fine. Let them head back together."

Justin shook his head. "No, we should make sure she's okay."

Cora smiled at him and shook the other boys off her arms. "I'm fine. I can walk."

Owen winked at me. "Come on, guys. We should head to my place. My mom made us a chocolate forest cake."

"My favorite!" Justin exclaimed. The other boys cheered with excitement. With the promise of food, they all took off running in the direction of Owen's house — away from the ocean.

Owen glanced back at me. I stared at him, unable to keep the hurt off my face. He paused, and for a moment I thought he was going to tell me something, but then he waved. "See you!" he called, running after his friends.

I wanted to cry. We still hadn't had a chance to have a real talk with Owen! But instead, I turned to Cora. "Can you walk?" I asked. "We have to get you home."

Cora put one arm over my shoulder and one arm over Shyanna's, and we hobbled along, moving slowly.

"Um, Rachel," Cora asked, "if something happens to my leg, does it affect my tail?"

"I have no idea," I snapped at her. "But if we don't get you home, you might not see Justin for a long time."

Cora stopped hobbling for a second. "You and Owen worked things out, right?"

I didn't answer.

"Oh, Rachel," Cora said, her voice cracking. "I'm so sorry. I got so caught up . . . "

"Flirting with Justin?" I said.

Cora dropped her head. "I'm sorry. I completely forgot to ask the other boys about what's going on with Owen."

"It's okay," I told her. "It's not your fault. Owen's problem is with me. Now let's get you home before you get into trouble."

Chapter Five

Thankfully, we made it home on time — and without running into any more sharks! The first thing my dad asked was how things had gone with Owen. I tried to convince him — and myself — that everything was fine. If Owen didn't want to be my best friend anymore, well, I had the mergirls and the Spirit Squad 2 and lots of new friends in Neptunia! It wasn't the end of the ocean!

The next morning, Dad gave me a hug and then headed off to see the Queen after breakfast. He was her singing instructor. I swam out into the yard just as Cora swam up. She had Jewel with her, and I couldn't help grinning at how cute my friend's baby sister was.

"Wow!" I said, admiring Cora's beautiful turquoise shell top. It made her colorful purple tail dazzle. "You look pretty beautiful to be babysitting."

"Thanks," Cora replied, blushing and looking away.

For a few minutes, we watched Jewel babble to a couple of sea starfish on the ocean ground. Finally Cora looked up at me. "So . . . are you sure you're not mad at me?" she asked. "I'm really sorry for not even trying to talk to the boys about Owen for you."

"It's okay," I told her. I didn't really want to talk about it. "How's your tail?"

"It seems fine. Maybe a little bruised where I hurt my leg but hardly noticeable."

"Good," I said. I grinned mischievously and sang: "Justin and Cora sitting in a tree . . ." I stopped quickly and smiled to show I was teasing.

Cora blushed again. “We’re friends!” she said but played with her hair nervously. “Actually he kind of asked me . . . us . . . to go shell hunting today. The boys are searching for a rare red dwarf mussel shell, the same shell Shyanna found.”

I glanced over at the sea starfish and Jewel. The starfish lifted an arm and watched us with the eye on the end.

“I told him I’d help. I know where to find one! Do you want to come?” Cora asked. “This time I’ll make sure we talk to Owen and get to the bottom of things.”

“When did Justin ask you along for the shell hunt?” I asked, trying to pretend I wasn’t hurt that Owen hadn’t invited me.

“When we were playing soccer,” Cora replied. She glanced down, and her cheeks flushed until they were as red as a lobster tail.

As much as I wanted to show how good I was at shell hunting too, I couldn’t face Owen again today. I didn’t want to risk more disappointment. Besides, he

hadn't even invited me. Things were weird, and I wasn't about to beg him to talk to me if he didn't want to.

I shook my head. "I really can't, Cora. I'm sorry. Why don't you ask Shyanna? She'll go," I said.

Cora shook her head. "She's with her mom today. They're taking a singing lesson with your dad and the Queen."

"Oh, that's right," I said. "I forgot. He's meeting them at Queen Kenna's."

Cora reached out and touched my arm. "Please don't be sad, Rachel. Owen still likes you. I know it. You should really come and talk to him. Clear things up once and for all."

I swam closer to watch baby Jewel and the sea starfish. "No. I don't want to deal with it today." I glanced at Cora. "Do you need me to babysit for you?" I wondered if that's why she really came over.

Cora shook her head. "No, Cassie said she would."

That made me feel a little bit better. At least Cora really did want me to go with her. She wasn't just trying to get me to look after her sister so she could go to shore and see Justin.

"I only have two hours again," Cora continued. "I have to hunt fast." She frowned. "I hate seeing you like this. You should come."

My bottom lip trembled. My feelings were already hurt, and I didn't want to keep trying to fix things if Owen didn't want to. Besides, it's not like he couldn't use mermaid magic to visit me if he wanted to.

At that moment Jewel stuck her finger out and the starfish squealed as it tried to scurry away. Jewel's mouth formed into an O, and she giggled. It was the cutest sound. Like Shyanna, sometimes I was envious of Cora's sisters.

"Why don't you ask Cassie to go to shore with you instead?" I suggested. "I don't mind babysitting Jewel. In fact, I'd love to. She's just what I need today. I can pretend to be a big sister."

"Trust me, baby sisters aren't all they're cracked up to be," Cora said. "You have so much freedom."

"Things always look bluer . . ." I started to say.

"On the other side of the ocean," Cora finished with a smile.

"Go show off for Justin," I said. The look on Cora's face made me giggle. She was glowing like plankton. "Be careful of those short-fin mako sharks."

Cora waved her hand. "They'll be long gone. Besides, you go to Platypus Island alone all the time."

"Yeah, because I've been doing it longer," I said. "I know all the shortcuts and hiding spots in case of danger. You haven't had your legs for very long."

Cora flipped her hair. "I'll swim by Cassie's cave on the way and see if she wants to join me. She's been wanting to meet our human friends." Cora swam down and kissed Jewel on top of her head. "You're sure you don't mind?"

"Go on," I said. "You don't have a lot of time if you're going to impress the boys with your mad hunting skills!"

Cora swam off, an extra wiggle in her tail.

* * *

Baby Jewel was adorable. We played with the starfish, and then I took her inside for a snack. She ended up taking a nap right at the kitchen table! When she woke up, I took her to Walrus Waterpark. I made sure to leave a note for Cora at my cave so she'd know where to find us.

Cora could say what she wanted about being a big sister, but playing with Jewel definitely kept my mind off Owen. I chased her down the slide and pushed her in the baby swing. Later we were joined in the park by a young merboy and mergirl from nearby caves. They were obviously best friends — I could tell by the way they played and finished each other's sentences. Seeing them, my heart ached a little. They reminded me of Owen and me.

When I looked down at my shell watch, I was shocked how much time had passed. I glanced around the water park. Cora should be back by now. I kept an eye on the entrance to the water park, but there was no sign of her.

I started to get worried, remembering the sharks. I pulled my shell phone out and called Cassie's cave. She answered right away. "Are you guys back already? Is Cora with you?" I asked.

"Cora? No. She went to shore to play with those human boys," Cassie said.

"I thought you went with her?" I said.

"My mom wouldn't let me," Cassie answered.

I tried not to sound nervous as I said goodbye and hung up. My shell phone rang almost immediately.

"Rachel. It's Mrs. Bass," Cora's mother said when I picked up. "Is Cora with you? She needs to get home right away."

I glanced around, but there was still no sign of Cora. Where was she, and what was taking her so long?

Chapter Six

"Um, Cora isn't back yet, Mrs. Bass," I said into the shell phone. "But I'm sure she's on her way. I know she was going shell hunting. She probably just lost track of time." I didn't mention the sharks we'd seen the day before — or that Cora had gone shell hunting alone. "Do you want me to bring Jewel home?"

As if on cue, Jewel started to cry, signaling that playtime was over. I tried to shush her and gave her a reassuring smile.

"Yes, please," Mrs. Bass replied. "I'll see you soon."

I hung up the shell phone, rocked Jewel gently in my arms, and swam toward Cora's cave. She was asleep by the time we arrived. Cora's mom and dad swam out of their cave to meet me.

"Still no sign of Cora?" Mrs. Bass asked as she took Jewel from my arms. "She's with Cassie, isn't she?"

I didn't answer, and her mom handed Jewel to her husband. "Can you put Jewel in her crib, dear?" she asked.

Cora's dad nodded and smiled at me, then took the baby from his wife and swam back inside.

"I'm worried, Rachel," Mrs. Bass said. "Cora isn't usually late. She knows how strict I am about curfews. This isn't like her." She glanced at their cave. "We're supposed to visit Grandmermaid." She looked down at the large shell watch on her wrist. "She knows it's important to me to be on time."

"Well . . . you know how competitive Cora is," I said. "Maybe she had trouble finding the shell but wanted to show off a little."

I thought about the mako sharks, and my worry started to grow. I didn't say anything about Cora's crush on Justin and how that might have distracted her from her curfew. And I didn't mention that Cassie hadn't gone with her or that Cora had hurt her leg the day before. I didn't know if mermaid legs healed quickly or not. If she got stuck onshore it would be a disaster. I should have made sure Cassie was allowed to go before I offered to babysit Jewel.

"I'll go and see what's going on," I told Cora's mom. "I'm sure she's on her way back, but I can go meet her, just to make sure nothing's wrong."

"Is Cassie with her?" her mom asked again.

I couldn't lie. I shook my head, and Cora's mom frowned. "I'll go with you," she said. "I don't want you going off on your own too. I really wish Cora hadn't done that. She certainly won't be allowed to in the future." Her eyebrows creased together, and her voice was firm.

The two of us had just started swimming toward the exit of Neptunia Castle when, in a whirl of bubbles and motion, Cora raced inside. Her eyes were wide, and when she glanced at me they grew even bigger.

"Cora Bass," her mom said. "You are late. You had us worried." I knew Mrs. Bass was relieved Cora was okay, but that wouldn't get Cora out of the big trouble she was in.

"Rachel —" Cora started to say.

"Cora," her mom interrupted, "come back to the cave with me right now." She motioned for her daughter to start moving. "You are not going to leave our cave until it's time to go back to school." Mrs. Bass glanced at me. "Thank you for looking after Jewel. Now move it, Cora."

"But I have to tell Rachel —" Cora began.

"Cave," Mrs. Bass said firmly, pointing in the direction of their home. "And no shell phone and no

talking to your friends for the rest of the weekend. You'll wait until school."

"But . . ." Cora looked at me, her eyes wide. There was an expression on her face that I couldn't quite figure out.

"No," her mother said, crossing her arms until Cora started to swim.

Just before they disappeared from sight, Cora turned back to look at me over her shoulder. "I HAVE SOMETHING IMPORTANT TO TELL YOU," she mouthed.

I frowned. I was as curious as a catfish, but I'd have to wait until Cora's punishment was over to find out what was so important. What had she discovered?

Chapter Seven

I needed someone to talk to, so I swam over to Shyanna's cave, but she wasn't there. I swam back to Cassie's next, but she was gone too.

I sighed. It didn't really matter. After all, it was Cora I needed to talk to. How would I ever last until her punishment ended? School was two whole days away. I needed to know what she'd learned *now.*

Had Cora talked to Owen? Did she know why he was avoiding me? Was he sick? Had I done something to offend him? I worried and fretted and wondered if there was any way he and I could go back to being best friends. My head kept whispering that I should go ask him, but my heart was too afraid to hear his answer. The thought of losing him was more than I could bear.

I swam by Walrus Waterpark and saw some merkids from merschool, but I couldn't talk to them about my problem. None of them understood how important my friendship with Owen was. No one in Neptunia knew me like Shyanna and Cora.

Finally I swam back to my cave, hoping my dad would be home and could help me figure things out. I swam into the kitchen and saw a note waiting on the counter: "Hi, Rachel. The Queen has asked for an extra private lesson for her sister who's visiting. I'll be home a little late."

I was too distracted to eat, so I swam to my room and stretched out on the bed. I closed my eyes, but all I could see was Owen turning away from me. My heart felt empty. I missed being his friend so much.

Suddenly, out of nowhere, a voice whispered, "Rachel?"

My eyes popped open, and I flipped around in a circle. "Hello?" I called into the water. "Who's there?" My heart was hammering in my chest.

A flash of purple streaked past me into my room. I screamed in shock as a hand reached out and grabbed mine.

"Rachel, it's me," Cora said. She flipped around, moving so quickly she created a wake of water in my room.

"Cora?" I yelled, feeling angry that she'd scared me and embarrassed that I hadn't recognized her voice. "What are you doing here? I thought you couldn't leave your house. Did you sneak out? Oh my gosh, you're going to be in trouble."

"No," Cora said, "but I am in a hurry." She finally stopped spinning and moving. "Mom told me I could swim over as fast as I could when I told her how important this was."

"What?" I cried. "What's wrong?"

"She wouldn't even let me use my shell phone," Cora continued. "'You have five minutes to go to Rachel's and get back home,' she told me."

My heart thumped like a sea otter's tail on the ocean floor. "What?" I cried. "What is it?"

"I don't have long. I have to swim straight home," Cora said.

I grabbed her arm, worried my head would explode if she didn't tell me soon. "Cora! Tell me!"

She put her hand on top of mine. "I know what's wrong with Owen."

My stomach dropped like a bird diving for fish.

"He isn't mad at you at all," Cora said.

"He's not?" I said, feeling a brief moment of relief.

Cora shook her head, and her hair shimmered and flowed in the water.

"Then what is it?" I demanded. "What's wrong?"

Cora finally stopped moving around and froze, staring right at me. "He's moving."

Chapter Eight

"He's what?" I said, but it wasn't really a question.

Cora dropped her gaze. She glanced around my room, pretending to be fascinated by the posters of the King and Queen on my cave wall. "Moving. You know, like when you moved to Neptunia from Caspian. But humans have to pack up all their things and rent trucks and drive for hours. It takes so much longer to get around on land."

"I know what moving is," I said quietly. "But where is Owen going? It's not far, right?"

Cora's bottom lip popped out, and she shook her head. "Justin told me it's not good, Rachel. Not good at all. Owen's dad got offered a new job — a good one."

I closed my eyes, preparing for the worst.

"I guess his dad is pretty sure they're going to go," Cora continued. "He's making his final decision soon. Justin said Owen refuses to talk about it with them."

All of a sudden things made sense to me. Why Owen was avoiding me. Why he wouldn't talk to me. We were so close that he knew he couldn't hide his real feelings from me. If he was trying to avoid how he felt, of course he'd have to avoid me too. He didn't hate me!

"I have to go talk to Owen!" I exclaimed.

Cora nodded. "Yeah, you do." She reached out and squeezed my hand. "I'm sorry, Rachel, but I have to go. If I don't get home, I'll never be allowed to leave my cave again!" She hugged me quickly and swam off.

I wanted to go to shore right away, but to avoid getting in trouble, I waited for my dad to come home so I could ask permission. I regretted it, because Dad made me wait until morning. He didn't want me swimming off in the darkness. I knew he was right, but it was still torture. I barely slept a wink that night thinking about Owen moving away.

The next morning, Dad made me eat one of his mussel muffins, and then he swam with me to the exit of the castle on his way to go see Queen Kenna's sister again.

"Be careful, Rachel," Dad said as he swam away. "I'll see you at home tonight."

I nodded and took off. I swam so quickly that my fins were sore by the time I reached shore. I got my legs and ran as fast as they'd carry me up the beach and toward Owen's house. When I reached his front door, my lungs were almost bursting, working overtime breathing in oxygen from air instead of water.

His mom opened the door right away when I knocked, and as soon as she saw me, her eyes filled with tears. "Oh, Rachel," she said. "Owen's so upset. He's going to miss you so much."

"Then you really are moving?" I said. "For sure?"

Owen's mom nodded and stepped forward to hug me, resting her chin on top of my head. "You always smell so wonderful," she said, "almost like the ocean."

Owen's parents didn't know I was half-mermaid or that Owen had special merboy status. They had no clue he could visit Neptunia and swim in the ocean with his temporary merman tail the King and Queen of Neptunia had granted him. Telling them was forbidden.

I glanced up and saw Owen watching from the hallway. His face scrunched up into a frown, but I knew now he wasn't mad at me.

His mom let me go and turned to see him watching us. She squeezed my hand. "You two need to go take a walk on the beach and talk."

Owen nodded his head toward the door, and I followed him outside, holding my breath. It was weird the way the air tightened up my lungs. Breathing in water was so much easier.

"I've been so worried about you, Owen," I finally said after we'd walked down the grass toward the pebbled path that led to the beach.

"I know, and I'm so sorry, Rachel," Owen replied. "I've been a jerk." He paused and glanced at me. "I've been so mad. Not at you, obviously, but I couldn't tell you what was going on because I didn't want it to be real. I've been worried too. About leaving Platypus Island. My friends. I didn't want to face any of it."

Owen sighed so loudly I wondered if the mergirls could hear him in the ocean. "But the very worst part is leaving you. I guess I hoped if I didn't talk about it, if I pretended nothing was happening, it would all go away." He stopped and stared at me. "Can you ever forgive me?"

"Oh, Owen, of course!" I told him.

He bit his lip hard, as if trying not to cry. I didn't bother. Tears flowed down my cheeks, and I didn't even feel bad about wasting the mermaid magic in them. The King and Queen didn't like when we shed tears without collecting them, but I couldn't help it. I had no energy to look around for a shell to hold them. Owen's news was the worst. I wanted to grab his hand, pull him to the ocean, and make him stay a merboy forever, never to return to the land again.

"Come on," Owen said, pulling me farther down the beach.

We walked quickly and quietly, as if we could escape our problems by walking away from them. Owen stared up at some lovely yellow birds, shielding his eyes from the bright sun that beamed down, warming my skin. The birds chirped happily, and their wings gliding through the air reminded me of mermaids flipping through the water. The sun felt so hot on land. I had to adjust every time I came to shore.

"So, where are you moving?" I finally asked after we'd walked for a while. I slowed down, ready to face reality, but hoping he'd say his parents had at least decided to move somewhere close to the ocean.

Owen stopped walking, dropped his chin to his chest, and stared down at the flip-flops on his feet. "Montana."

I couldn't help it — I gasped. We'd been studying the geography of land in school, so I knew where he meant. "Montana? As in hundreds of miles away from the ocean?"

Owen nodded. "But that's not even the worst part."

Oh, no! I thought. *What could possibly be worse?*

"We're leaving in two days."

My breath stopped again, and I swallowed. "But that's so soon," I whispered. How could his family go so quickly? Owen and I were finally making up, and now we hardly had any time left to spend together.

Owen nodded. "Once my dad decided, they wanted him to start his new job right away." We both watched a seagull swoop down and steal something from the beach. "My dad says Montana is nice. No other state has as many species of mammals."

I wanted to shout at him that the ocean was much better, but I knew that would only make him feel worse. "Montana looked pretty in the pictures I saw at merschool," I said, trying to be happy for him.

"My dad says I can play on an ice hockey team," Owen added. "It's not the ocean, and it's frozen, but at least it's water. Right?" He bumped my shoulder with his, trying to make a joke.

I tried to smile.

"But the truth is, I'm going to miss the ocean," Owen continued. "And my friends." He glanced sideways. "But most of all you, Rachel. You're my best friend in the whole ocean. In the whole world!"

I looked away and fought back more tears. Owen was my best friend too. I couldn't imagine life without him.

Owen reached for my hand, and we walked like that for a minute. "Will I forget about you?" he asked quietly.

I swallowed a lump. "Yes," I whispered. "If you go too long without being in the ocean, without using your tail . . . the magic will fade. You'll forget all about being a merboy. You'll forget all about my life in the ocean. You might even forget all about me."

My insides felt like I'd been outside in the sun too long with my tail. Dried up and uncomfortable. I was so miserable I wanted to curl up in a ball and cry and cry.

"This is just so sad," I said. "Can you come to the ocean, Owen? Now? To see everyone and everything one more time?"

I needed him to come. I had to convince him to stay. It didn't have to be goodbye. He could come see all the beauty and stay. Owen loved splashing in the ocean with his gorgeous merboy tail. He loved to play with all the ocean creatures. He was as amazing as a merboy as he was as a human. Maybe even more!

Owen glanced back at his house. From where we stood, it looked so tiny and far away. I imagined him swimming away with me and never coming back. We'd take good care of him in the ocean. He could live in our cave. We had extra room.

"I have to text my mom," Owen said. He pulled out his phone, so different than my shell phone. "She'll worry if I'm gone too long. I'll tell her I'm going to your house."

I tried not to think about Owen's mom worrying about him or how she'd feel if he never came back. I had to convince him to stay. That was all that mattered.

Chapter Nine

We ran to the water, and Owen slid off his shoes, placing his phone on them and hiding everything in the bushes. As we dove into the ocean, Owen laughed as his beautiful red tail flipped out. I raced in front of him, diving into a wave, and he followed me, whooping as we passed a grumpy-looking walrus.

"It's so beautiful here," Owen said as we swam past schools of brilliantly colored fish and colored coral swaying in the water.

"It is," I agreed. "Maybe you could stay here. You know . . . forever?"

Owen didn't answer. Instead, he swam in circles and laughed with the dolphins as they nosed up beside him. We raced to Neptunia, and when we reached the castle, we spotted Shyanna at the park. She saw us too and a big smile warmed up her beautiful face.

"Owen!" Shy cried happily. She swam close and clapped her hands together. "I'm so glad to see you here. See, Rachel, I knew you two would make up. You're best friends!"

Just like that, my happiness bubble popped. All the sadness I'd been trying to hold in burst to the surface. "But it's terrible!" I exclaimed. "Everything is horrible!" I managed to hold in my tears knowing the Queen was close by.

"Rachel?" Shyanna patted my back and stroked my hair. She gave Owen a dirty look. "Owen, what did you do to Rachel?"

I shook my head and touched Owen's arm as his happy mood faded too. "No," I told Shyanna. "It's not

Owen's fault. It's just that his family is moving far away — to Montana. Away from the ocean."

Owen quickly explained about his dad getting a new job and how they'd be moving to Montana in two days. Shyanna's shoulders drooped, and she glanced at me with the kind of understanding a good friend has when someone she loves is hurting.

"You could live here!" I burst out. "You love being a merboy! You'd love merschool. You could spend as much time with the sea creatures as you want. And you could still do sports. Everything would be perfect! Stay, Owen. Stay with us!"

Owen's face and tail drooped, and I knew then that it was wrong to ask him that. My selfish bubble was burst.

"I'm sorry," I said. I remembered how my dad had felt when I'd wanted to leave the ocean to become human. Owen would miss his family. They would never know what had happened to him. He'd never be able to go to shore again. He'd miss his legs and being human.

"Let's not be upset," I said, forcing myself to think of Owen. "Let's make sure your last visit to the ocean is fun — not sad and mopey. Let's go see Cora. She can't leave her cave, because she was late coming from shore and worried her family. But her mom will let you in to say goodbye."

We swam off, and I tried to focus on being happy and enjoying the sea life around us. Even if Owen forgot his time with us when he'd been on land too long, I'd never forget him. He was my best friend — in the ocean or out of it.

Cora's mom made an exception because of the circumstances and let her play in her yard with us, so we chased her sisters and laughed with Owen. Before long, though, Owen glanced at me. "I should get back to shore," he told me. "I have a ton to do before we move."

I nodded as he hugged Cora and her sisters.

"Do you want me to come with you?" Shyanna asked, but I shook my head. She nodded, understanding that I needed to have my last moments with Owen alone.

Owen and I swam slowly and more quietly on our way back to shore than we had on the way to Neptunia. When we got close to shore I stopped. "I can't come all the way," I said, biting my lip and trying not to cry again. "Let's say goodbye here."

Owen nodded. "Thank you," he said softly. "For being the best friend I ever had. And giving me the best adventures. I'll never forget you, Rachel. No matter what. I may forget about your tail and the ocean. But I'll never forget you."

I smiled and bit my lip even harder, not trusting myself to say anything. Owen swam close and hugged me, then lightly kissed my cheek.

"Let's not say goodbye, let's say see you soon," he said. And with that, he swam away.

I watched as Owen reached shore, and his tail transformed back into legs. Then he grabbed his shoes and walked up the beach. He turned, staring back out at the water, but I dove down, flipping my tail on the water's surface to say goodbye.

Chapter Ten

The rest of the weekend dragged on. I spent most of my time alone in my room, thinking about Owen. On Monday when I swam to school, Cora and Shyanna swam to meet me and gave me big hugs.

"Losing Owen is hard," Cora said. "But you always have us. Friends until the end." She held out her hand, and I laid my hand on top. Shyanna laid her hand on top of mine.

"I made a wish last night," Shyanna told me. "I wished with all the mermaid magic I could muster.

I even looked through the Mermaid Magic Book of Cures."

"But we're not curing anything," I said.

"Maybe we are," she said mysteriously. My friends distracted me with chatter, but I still had a hole in my heart. I managed to drag myself through the school day, and then Shyanna and Cora swam home with me.

Dad was waiting in front of the cave. Someone treaded in the water beside him. Someone who looked an awful lot like Owen!

I squealed and swam forward. "Owen?" I cried. "What are you doing here?"

"He wanted to tell you in person," my dad said with a smile.

"Tell me what?" I asked, trying not to get my hopes up.

"I'm still moving, Rachel," Owen said. "But I snuck back to Neptuna this morning while my parents were packing. I figured it couldn't hurt to ask, so I talked to the King and Queen. I told them I was moving and wouldn't be near the ocean but that I'd be back someday. That I had to come back. I told them I loved Mermaid Kingdom and didn't want to ever forget my time here or being a merboy. I promised never to tell a human what I know. No matter what."

I held my breath in the water.

"And?" Shyanna practically screamed at him.

"And I won't forget!" Owen exclaimed. "I can come back someday. I won't lose my tail."

"They're not taking away your tail?" Shyanna asked. She flipped in a circle. "I knew it! A cure for a broken heart — that's what I wished for! I love mermaid magic!" She was so enthusiastic, we all laughed.

Cora swam closer to Owen. "This means we can stay in touch the way humans do! Justin told me about this thing called the Internet. You can see each other when you talk, even from long distances!"

Shyanna and I giggled, and Owen and my dad grinned. Cora glanced around and her cheeks turned bright pink. "What?" she asked.

"When did you talk to Justin?" Shyanna demanded.

"I, uh, kind of missed him this weekend," Cora said. "And I had a shell I wanted to give him, so I swam to shore before school."

Owen rescued her. "It's true. We really can use the Internet to talk. It won't be the same, but it's better than nothing. You can get the guys to help you." He glanced at Cora then and winked. "I'm sure Justin will be happy to help you girls stay in touch."

We all laughed at the uncomfortable look on Cora's face.

Owen turned back to me. "I have to get home. We're leaving tonight, and I have a lot to do. I told my mom I wouldn't be gone long. But I wanted to tell you I won't forget you. As long as I never tell another human about merlife, I won't have to forget anything!"

"Just like you promised," I whispered.

The mergirls and my dad all grinned, and then it was my turn to blush.

"Come on," I said to my friends. I couldn't wipe the grin off my face.

Shyanna and Cora joined hands, and Owen grabbed mine as we all swam off together. Dad watched from the front of our cave, smiling and waving goodbye.

When we got closer to shore, Shyanna and Cora hung back a little, and I swam slowly with Owen into the shallow water. It was sad saying goodbye again, but knowing we would never forget each other made a big difference.

Owen turned to me and grinned. "I'll come back when I can," he said. "I promise, I'll be back."

"I know," I told him, my insides dancing happily. We hugged each other so tightly I couldn't breathe.

Owen let go first. "I'll see you on the Internet. I'll be in Montana and ready to talk in one week."

"You bet you will," I told him, excited to learn how the Internet worked.

Owen swam away quickly but turned back before his legs appeared. "I'll miss you, Rachel Marlin!" he called. "You're a great best friend."

"I'll miss you too!" I called back.

Shyanna and Cora swam to me then, and we watched Owen climb out of the water, off to his new adventures in Montana with his sturdy earth legs.

My friends each grabbed one of my hands, and we swam off together, back to our home in the ocean. I knew we'd see Owen again.

Legend of Mermaids

These creatures of the sea have many secrets. Although people have believed in mermaids for centuries, nobody has ever proven their existence. People all over the world are attracted to the mysterious mermaids.

The earliest mermaid story dates back to around 1000 BC in an Assyrian legend. A goddess loved a human man but killed him accidentally. She fled to the water in shame. She tried to change into a fish, but the water would not let her hide her true nature. She lived the rest of her days as half-woman, half-fish.

Later, the ancient Greeks whispered tales of fishy women called sirens. These beautiful but deadly beings lured sailors to their graves. Many sailors feared or respected mermaids because of their association with doom.

Note: This text was taken from The Girl's Guide to Mermaids: Everything Alluring about These Mythical Beauties *by Sheri A. Johnson (Capstone Press, 2012). For more mermaid facts, be sure to check this book out!*

Talk It Out

1. Losing a friend is hard, even if you plan to stay in touch. Imagine yourself in Rachel's position. Talk about how you would feel when Owen revealed his secret.

2. Rachel's friends promise to help her find out what's going on with Owen. Talk about a time one of your friends helped you with something. What was it, and how did things turn out?

3. Friendship is a special type of love. What qualities make a good friend? How are those qualities shown in this story?

4. What would you have done if you were Owen? Would you have told Rachel about your family's plans to move right away? Do you think he was right to wait?

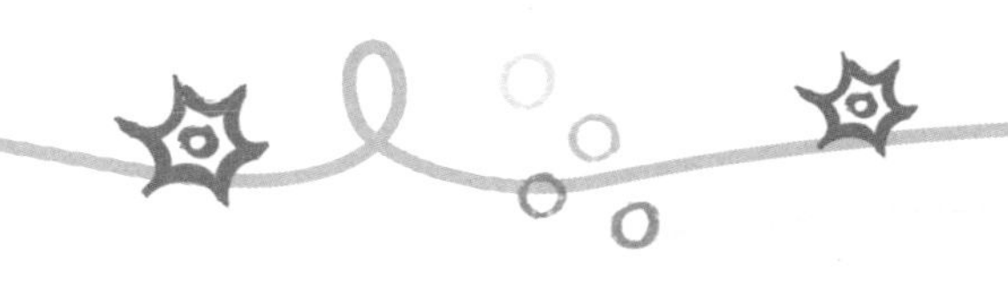

Write It Down

1. Pretend you are Owen. Write a paragraph about your new life in Montana. How are things different? What do you like about it?

2. Rachel and Owen decide to keep in touch using the Internet once he moves away. Pretend you are either Rachel or Owen and write an email to the other person.

3. Keeping secrets can be hard on a friendship. Has a friend ever kept a secret from you? Have you ever kept a secret from a friend? Write a paragraph about how you felt and how you dealt with the situation.

4. How do you think Rachel and Owen's relationship will change when he no longer lives by the ocean? Write a chapter that continues this story.

About the Author

Janet Gurtler has written numerous well-received YA books. Mermaid Kingdom is her debut series for younger readers. She lives in Calgary, Alberta, near the Canadian Rockies, with her husband, son, and a chubby Chihuahua named Bruce. Gurtler does not live in an igloo or play hockey, but she does love maple syrup and says "eh" a lot.

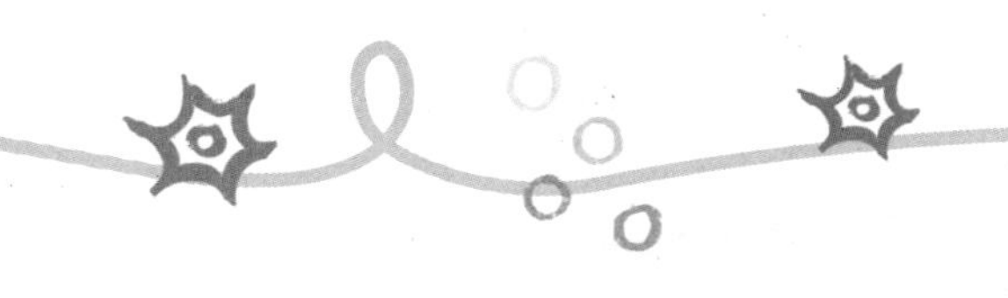

About the Illustrator

Katie Wood fell in love with drawing when she was very small. Since graduating from Loughborough University School of Art and Design in 2004, she has been living her dream working as a freelance illustrator. From her studio in Leicester, England, she creates bright and lively illustrations for books and magazines all over the world.

Mermaid
KINGDOM

Dive in and get swept away!

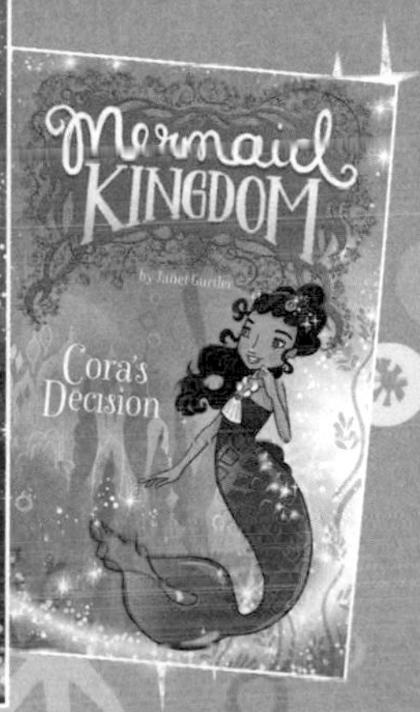

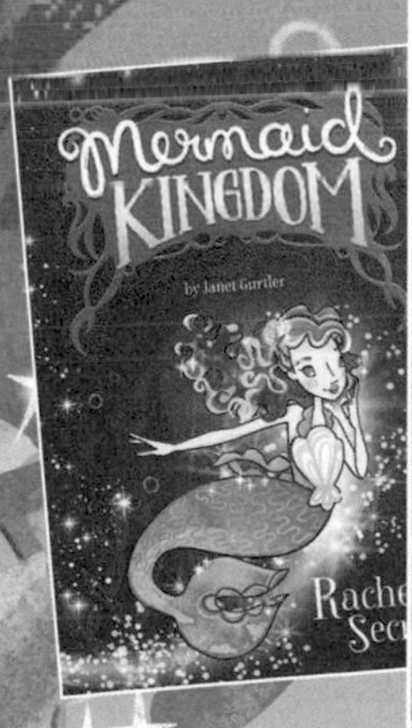